THE
BOOK REPORT
FROM THE
BLACK LAGOON®

by Mike Thaler
Illustrated by Jared Lee

SCHOLASTIC INC.

New York   Toronto   London   Auckland
Sydney   Mexico City   New Delhi   Hong Kong

This book is dedicated to all the kids
who love to read.
—M.T.

To Barry Lee
—J.L.

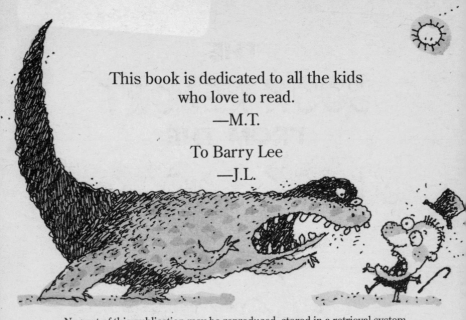

10 Book PACK ISBN: 978-0-545-29046-3
Single Book ISBN: B-OK5-29046-5

12 11 10 9 8 7 6 5 4 3 2 1   10 11 12 13 14 15/0

Printed in the U.S.A.   75
First printing, October 2010

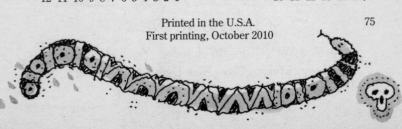

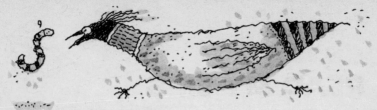

CONTENTS

CHAPTER 1
READ MY LIPS

Mrs. Green wants us to write a book report—in two weeks—on a "real" book! Not a picture book, not a comic book . . . but a "real" book with *chapters*! I asked her if I could write a movie report or a video game report. She said, "No!"

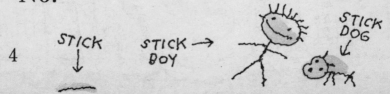

I'm a slow reader. It takes me three minutes to read a STOP sign.

I'll never do it. I'm doomed.

CHAPTER 2
SLEEPING ON THE JOB

 ← TEA

Mrs. Green marches us to the library to pick out our books. Mrs. Beamster is there to help us. I don't think she can help me. I'm beyond help.

"What are you interested in, Hubie?"

MRS. BEAMSTER, MAY I GO TO LUNCH EARLY?

THIS ISN'T MY CUP OF TEA.

"I'm interested in not writing a book report."

"What subjects do you like? There are books on just about everything: baseball, football, auto racing, history, mystery, and even spies."

"I'm interested in sleeping."

Mrs. Beamster smiles. She goes to the shelf and brings back *Rip Van Winkle*. It's about a guy who falls asleep for twenty years. He should get a new alarm clock.

Next she brings me *Sleeping Beauty*, about a princess who falls asleep for a hundred years, until a prince comes along and kisses her. On the lips. *Echh!* Talk about morning mouth.

← BUZZZ

RIP AWAKE →

PRINCESS AFTER A LONG NAP →

After going through shelves of books, I finally pick *Robin Hood*. Mrs. Beamster says it's exciting and even has a few pictures. I like pictures.

9

CHAPTER 3

BOOK TALK

On the bus, all the kids are talking about their book reports. *Boring*. Eric says he's going to do the phone book. He must be kidding—I've got his number. Freddy has a cookbook—that's a recipe for disaster. Doris chose a book about ballet—that will keep her on her toes. Randy's got a book about all the planets— far-out. And Derek's reading a thesaurus—is that about dinosaurs?

MAYBE I SHOULD HAVE GOT A BOOK ON ROBINS INSTEAD OF ROBIN HOOD.

11

"What's your book, Hubie?" asks everyone.

I take out my book. It's big. It's heavy. It's full of words. I put it back in my book bag.

"Hey," says Eric, "I saw the movie. It's about a guy in green pajamas who lives in the forest and shoots arrows."

"Is that it?" I ask.

"That's it," says Eric.

I wonder why it took the author so many words to say that.

HOW TO READ

YOU'RE DOING A FINE JOB.

13

CHAPTER 4
THE WRONG FOOT

When I get home, I go straight to my room and close the door. No milk, no chocolate chip cookies, no video games. I open my book. In front it says "Table of Contents."

There are lots of chapters and 238 pages. If I read a page every 20 minutes, that's 4,760 minutes. 60 minutes into 4,760 is more than 79 hours. I'll be an old man when I finish this book. Maybe I do need a chocolate chip cookie.

CHAPTER 5
A COOKIE, NOT A BOOKIE

COOKIE

CRUMBS

"Could I have another cookie, Mom?"

"Hubie, you've already had twelve. You're going to ruin your appetite."

"Just one more, Mom."

"Is something bothering you?"

"I have to read a book."

"So?"

"A *big* book."

"So?"

"A book with 50,400 words."

"How do you know how many words are in the book?"

YOU CAN DO IT, HUBIE.

← DIRT

"I counted them."

"Hubie, a book is not a math problem. A book is an adventure. The longer the better. When you're reading a good book, you don't *want* it to end."

"Could I have another cookie, Mom?"

I'LL SETTLE FOR A CRUMB.

BUT, MOM.

17

VACUUM CLEANER →

CHAPTER 6
ONCE AROUND THE BLOCK

I go back to my room. I pick up the book. Heavy. Maybe I should clean up my room before I start. It would be easier to read in a neat room. So I straighten my room.

"Hubie, it's time for dinner!"

Saved by the smell.

After dinner, I help Mom wash the dishes. I take out the trash. I take my dog for a walk.

I start to vacuum the rug.

"Hubie, you're acting very strange. Are you sick?"

Mom feels my forehead.

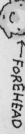

← FOREHEAD

"You are a little hot. What's wrong?"

"You've heard of writer's block. Well, I have reader's block."

"Hubie, maybe you should take a hot shower, put on your pajamas, and go to sleep."

CHAPTER 7
CLIMBING MOUNT NEVEREST

That night I have a bookmare. I'm standing in front of a giant mountain. A mountain of words. I start to slowly climb. Suddenly, there's a rumbling and the whole mountain shakes. It's an avalanche! I'm buried in words. I wake up under my pillow. I run to Mom's room. Luckily, she's up reading.

LADDERS

RUMBLE

RUN!

"What's wrong, Hubie?"
"I can't sleep."
"Well, get back in bed. I'll make you some hot chocolate and come in and read to you."

CHAPTER 8
A STRAIGHT ARROW

Mom reads to me from *my* book—*Robin Hood.* The first chapter tells how Robin becomes an outlaw. He's betrayed by an evil king. I want to stay up and see what happens, but my eyes slowly close.

When I wake up, my book is on the nightstand and Mom has put a beautiful green bookmark in it. I open to that page and start reading.

"Hubie, it's time for breakfast. You're going to be late for school."

NECK →

ROBIN HOOD IS A PAIN IN THE NECK.

"Oh, Mom, can't I just finish this chapter?"

I get dressed in record time and run to the bus stop. I read while I'm waiting for the bus. It comes much too soon. I keep reading and almost trip while getting on the bus. I sit down next to Eric.

"Hey, Hubie, I heard a really funny joke."

"Later—I'm reading."

WOW!

SCHOOL BUS

THOMAS JEFFERSON

CHAPTER 9
HOOKED ON
THE BOOK

I tuck my book on my lap and read during class.

"Hubie, who was the third president of the United States?"

"The Sheriff of Nottingham."

HUBIE, I WANT TO SEE YOU AFTER CLASS.

CAN I BRING MY BOOK WITH ME?

OH, NO.

BOOK ON LAP

I read during recess. I play right field. My mitt makes a good book stand. Luckily, nobody hits a ball out here.

"Hubie, do you want to come over after school and play video games? I got the latest one, *Cage Fighting with Dinosaurs*."

"Sorry, Eric. Robin is in trouble. I have to see what happens."

CAPTAIN, HUBIE'S NOT TAKING OUR CALLS.

CHAPTER 10
IN THE GROOVE

And so it goes.

"Hubie, it's time for dinner."

"I'm reading, Mom."

"Hubie, your favorite TV show is on."

"I'm reading, Mom."

"Hubie, it's time to go to sleep."

"I'm reading, Mom."

I've become "Mr. I'm Reading, Mom"! But things are working out for Robin Hood.

RING! RING!

YOUR PHONE IS RINGING.

TV OFF

CHAPTER 11
THE FINISH LINE

I finished the book and wrote my report. It was long. It was good. I got an A+. My first one. Maybe I'll be a writer one day . . . if I can find the time between reading books. I'll be busy because there are millions of books to read.

GOOD JOB!

A+

I CAN'T WAIT TO TELL MOM.

Get more monster-sized laughs from

The Black Lagoon®

#18: The Author Visit from the Black Lagoon®

AUTHOR'S NOTE:

Every book is a time machine, a flying carpet, a passport to the most powerful nation in the world ... your imagi-nation!

Mike Thaler